Howie Schneider

G. P. PUTNAM'S SONS

TO SUSIE, SOPHIA AND JACOB

G. P. PUTNAM'S SONS

A division of Penguin Young Readers Group.

Published by The Penguin Group.

Penguin Group (USA) Inc., 375 Hudson Street, New York, NY 10014, U.S.A.

Penguin Group (Canada), 90 Eglinton Avenue East, Suite 700, Toronto, Ontario, Canada M4P 2Y3 (a division of Pearson Penguin Canada Inc.). Penguin Books Ltd, 80 Strand, London WC2R 0RL, England. Penguin Ireland, 25 St. Stephen's Green, Dublin 2, Ireland (a division of Penguin Books Ltd.). Penguin Group (Australia), 250 Camberwell Road, Camberwell, Victoria 3124, Australia (a division of Pearson Australia Group Pty Ltd). Penguin Books India Pvt Ltd, 11 Community Centre, Panchsheel Park, New Delhi – 110 017, India. Penguin Group (NZ), Cnr Airborne and Rosedale Roads, Albany, Auckland 1310, New Zealand (a division of Pearson New Zealand Ltd). Penguin Books (South Africa) (Pty) Ltd, 24 Sturdee Avenue, Rosebank, Johannesburg 2196, South Africa. Penguin Books Ltd, Registered Offices: 80 Strand, London WC2R 0RL, England.

Published simultaneously in Canada. Manufactured in China by South China Printing Co. Ltd.

Design by Gunta Alexander. Text set in Bradley Extended.

Library of Congress Cataloging-in-Publication Data

Schneider, Howie, 1930– Wilky the White House cockroach / Howie Schneider.

p. cm. Summary: Bored with life in the back of Oscar's Pizza Palace in Washington, D.C., a young cockroach sets off in a pizza box in search of adventure, only to become a very unwelcome guest at the White House. [1. Cockroaches—Fiction. 2. White House (Washington, D.C.)—Fiction. 3. Adventure and adventurers—Fiction. 4. Washington (D.C.)—Fiction. 5. Humorous stories.] I. Title. PZ7.S3633Wil 2006 [E]—dc22 2005026897 ISBN 0-399-24388-7

1 3 5 7 9 10 8 6 4 2

First Impression

Wilky was a young cockroach who lived with his large family behind a crack in the wall at Oscar's Pizza Palace in Washington, D.C., not far from the White House.

Oscar didn't bother them as long as they stayed on the floor in the back.

"If I ever catch a bug up on the countertop," Oscar said, "I'll crush him to a pulp." But Wilky could smell the hot pizzas coming out of the oven all day long.

"Don't go up there, Wilky," pleaded his mother. "You'll end up like your uncle Julius, a stain on the wall."

Uncle Julius used to return from his adventures with exciting stories of all the close calls he had. "Don't be afraid to be afraid," he would tell them.

Wilky wanted more than anything to be like his uncle Julius. He even wore a pimento cap just like he did, risky as that was for a cockroach.

So Wilky went up.

He hid behind a tin of grated cheese and watched as Oscar slid a sizzling-hot mushroom and sausage pizza into a large cardboard box, almost under Wilky's nose.

"Go get it, kid," he could hear Uncle Julius saying. "You only live once."

So Wilky jumped in.

Oscar closed the box. The sudden darkness made Wilky feel at home. It was always the light that brought trouble for a cockroach.

He couldn't believe how good hot, melted cheese tasted. He ate fast because, as Uncle Julius had often told him, with eating this good, a light was coming soon.

And it came swiftly, as the box was flung open with a cry to strike terror in the hearts of cockroaches the world over. In every language on Earth it meant the same thing:

"Squash him!"

Wilky pulled himself out of the melted cheese and threw himself off the table.

He started running toward the wall without looking back. The carpet was thick and hard to run on.

He could tell from the enormous shadow that suddenly stretched across the floor that he was in big trouble.

"Head for a corner," he remembered Uncle Julius saying. "They can't get a shoe into a corner."

But this room had no corners. This was the Oval Office.
This was where the President of the United States worked.
Wilky was afraid his first adventure was soon going to
be his last.

A door flew open
and lots of people ran in.

"There's a cockroach in the
White House!" the President shouted.

"A cockroach in *my* White House,"
cried the First Lady. "I'll never live this down."

Wilky noticed they had left the door open.

So he ran out.

These guys act like they never saw a cockroach before, thought Wilky.

He was startled when part of the wall near him slid open, revealing a small room. People came running out.

So Wilky ran in.

More people came running in after him, and the wall closed again.

"I'd like to get a look at this bug," said the Chairman of the Senate Tiny Problems Committee.

"Let's hear what the President has to say at this emergency Cabinet meeting," said the Minister of Dark and Dirty Places.

When the wall opened again, Wilky entered the Cabinet room with the others, riding on the polka-dot dress of the Secretary of Interiors.

The President was furious. "I do not intend to be the first President to have a cockroach in his White House," he bellowed. "Especially with the state dinner we're planning tonight in honor of the French President and his wife."

He glared around the table at the Bug Czar, the Minister of Creepy Crawlies, and the Secretary of Small Creatures.

"FIND THAT COCKROACH!" he roared. "And step on it!"

"Let's check the kitchen," said the Bug Czar. "Cockroaches love kitchens."

Cool, a kitchen, thought Wilky as he clung to the Secretary's dress while everyone ran down the back stairs.

The kitchen staff was busy preparing for the state dinner.

"Out!" shouted the chef. "Out of my kitchen."

"Special orders from the President," said the officials. Wilky jumped from the dress onto a table and looked for cover.

Wilky spotted some olive pits. Using all his strength, he nudged each pit off the table onto the floor, where they started rolling off in every direction with officials in hot pursuit. Even the kitchen staff joined in.

Wilky watched from the top of an open box of raisins as they went stomping all over the kitchen after the olive pits. He was exhausted.

So he dropped down for a nap.

All the knowledge and advanced technology of the strongest
nation on Earth was brought into play to find the little cockroach.
"This bug's goose is cooked," said the Director of the FBI.

But by the time the state dinner for the French President and his wife was set to begin, Wilky was still at large.

The President put on a happy face, but you could tell he was concerned.

The dinner was a huge success. The kitchen staff started preparing the dessert of rice pudding with raisins.

Wilky awoke to find himself lying on a soft bed of warm rice with his head irresistibly close to a small pool of heavy cream. He knew what Uncle Julius would have done in this situation. "Never pass up a chance to eat," he'd say, "there may not be another."

So Wilky nibbled.

The French President's wife's scream brought the dinner to an abrupt halt, and once again Wilky found himself running for his life.

The next morning at his regularly scheduled press briefing, the President was asked about rumors of a cockroach in the White House.

"Mr. President," asked a reporter, "isn't it true that the White House is infested with cockroaches, one of which viciously attacked the French President's wife in an attempt to destroy our relations with France?"

"As far as we know," the President replied, trying hard to control himself, "we are dealing with a lone cockroach here. There's no evidence of an organized plot."

Back at Oscar's Pizza Palace, even Wilky's family heard the news conference.

"Oh no!" cried Wilky's mother. "It's my Wilky! I know it is."

Hordes of cousins, brothers, sisters, and friends let out a loud cheer: "Way to go, Wilk!"

But the truth was, Wilk was running out of ways to go. It seemed now as if everyone was after him.

"You've got six legs to their two," he heard Uncle Julius saying. "So use them."

So he did.

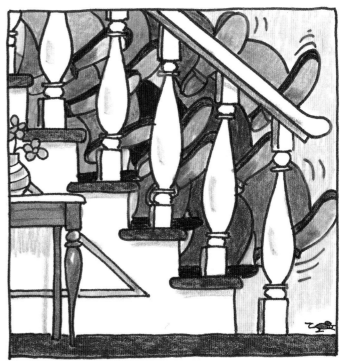

The President met with the leaders of Congress.

"My friends, I'm sorry to report that we have not caught the cockroach. Believe me, this is one smart, tough little bug," he told them. "He has earned the respect and admiration of us all. I suggest we offer him a truce. Trust me, it will cost much less to feed him than it will to catch him. Personally I can't wait to meet him."

The Secret Service broke in to report that they had the little bug cornered somewhere on the world map in the War Room, and the Exterminator General was on his way.

"Good luck, Mr. President," the leaders called after him as he rushed out of the room.

Wilky was posing as a small island off the coast of Siberia. His pimento cap blended in with all the red pins. When he saw the Exterminator General enter the room in full uniform, he began to tremble.

Uncle Julius had always warned him to stay away from exterminators.

"They're hired killers," he said. "They do it for the money."

"Wait!" said the President, who had just arrived. "Don't spray! I'll handle this."

"Little bug," he said, turning to address the map. "Wherever you are, let's stop this madness. You win! Let's make a truce. We can use a smart bug like you. You will be the White House Cockroach, representing all the bugs in America. We'll supply you with everything a cockroach could want. And no one will bother you. I give you my word. What d'ya say?"

Wow! thought Wilky. Wait until Mama hears this . . . the White House Cockroach. The President was offering him a better deal than the family had at Oscar's.

But could Wilky trust him? He didn't know what Uncle Julius would have done in this situation. Maybe Mama was right, he thought. I'll be squashed like Uncle Julius was. But he was tired of running. And besides, there was no place left to run.

So Wilky came down.

Together the President and his new White House official walked through a relieved crowd eager to applaud this remarkable truce between man and bug.

The President was true to his word. Wilky had everything a cockroach could want . . . except the most important thing: his family. The President's wife refused to allow the thousands of Wilky's relatives to visit him at the White House.

"It's not an adventure," he could hear Uncle Julius say, "if you can't tell the family about it."

When the President heard about Wilky's dilemma, he was very upset. He had given his word to grant the little bug his every wish.

So Wilky went home. And for the rest of their lives the family enjoyed hot pizzas and Secret Service protection courtesy of the President of the United States.

"Well done, kid," he thought he heard Uncle Julius saying.